For Gabriel

Thomas the Tortoise

GRAHAM JEFFERY

Crown Publishers, Inc.
New York

Published in the United States by Crown Publishers, Inc., 225 Park Avenue
South, New York, New York 10003.
Published in Great Britain by Methuen Children's Books Ltd.
CROWN is a trademark of Crown Publishers, Inc.
Manufactured in Hong Kong
Library of Congress Cataloging-in-Publication Data
Jeffrey, Graham.
     Thomas, the tortoise/by Graham Jeffrey.
         p.   cm.
     Summary: Feeling sad about being the slowest animal in the garden, Thomas
the tortoise decides to go into his shell and never come out.
     [1. Turtles—Fiction. 2. Animals—Fiction.] I. Title.
PZ7. J3664Th 1988
[E]—dc19   88-7098   CIP   AC
     ISBN 0-517-57043-2

     10 9 8 7 6 5 4 3 2 1
First Edition

Thomas the tortoise was the slowest thing in the garden.

He was slower than the roller William pushed.

He was slower than Fido, or Tibby the cat.

And he was much slower than the birds, which flew in the sky.

Thomas was the slowest thing in the whole garden.

He was so slow,   he took ages

just to come   on to the page.

And when he did, he just stayed there,
looking sadly at the flowers and the trees and the
sun, and thinking it was time for a piece of lettuce.

One day, William was sitting on the bench, eating his sandwiches. "Hello," he said to Thomas. "You look sad. What's the matter?"
But Thomas was so sad he went back into his shell and wouldn't come out, even when William gave him a piece of cake.

"What's wrong, Thomas?" said William.
"You shouldn't be sad. It's a nice day and the sun is shining, and if you like I'll give you my sandwiches as well."

But Thomas only started to cry. And big tears
rolled on to the grass. "Why are you crying?"
asked William. "Is it because you are slow?"

And when Thomas went on crying, William picked him up gently and took him to the potting shed.

"I know just the thing for you," he said.
And Thomas poked his head out of his shell and said,
"Wheels! What do I want with wheels?"

"Just you wait and see," said William.
"First I take an old box, then I take some wheels.

"Then I take a hammer and some nails."

Thomas looked very pleased. "Is that for me?" he said.
"It certainly is," said William.

And William put Thomas in the box
and pulled him all around the garden.

"Of course," said Thomas happily,
"I'm still not as quick as Fido or Tibby . . .

"and I'll never be as quick as the birds in the sky.

"But I'm happy where I am, here in my garden, and best of all . . .

"I'm having fun with my friends."